HANDS-ON HISTORY

HOMES

BRING THE PAST ALIVE WITH 30 GREAT PROJECTS

Consulting editors Rachel Halstead and Struan Reid

southwater

This edition is published by Southwater

Southwater is an imprint of Anness Publishing Ltd
Hermes House, 88–89 Blackfriars Road, London SE1 8HA
tel. 020 7401 2077; fax 020 7633 9499
www.southwaterbooks.com; info@anness.com
© Anness Publishing Ltd 2003

This edition distributed in the UK by
The Manning Partnership Ltd
tel. 01225 478 444; fax 01225 478 440
sales@manning-partnership.co.uk

This edition distributed in the USA and Canada by
National Book Network
tel. 301 459 3366; fax 301 459 1705
www.nbnbooks.com

This edition distributed in Australia by Pan Macmillan Australia
tel. 1300 135 113; fax 1300 135 103
customer.service@macmillan.com.au

This edition distributed in New Zealand by The Five Mile Press
(NZ) Ltd
tel. (09) 444 4144; fax (09) 444 4518
fivemilenz@clear.net.nz

Publisher: Joanna Lorenz
Managing Editor: Linda Fraser
Editors: Leon Gray, Sarah Uttridge
Designer: Sandra Marques/Axis Design Editions Ltd
Jacket Design: Dean Price
Photographers: Paul Bricknell and John Freeman
Illustrators: Rob Ashby, Julian Baker, Andy Beckett, Mark Beesley,
Mark Bergin, Richard Berridge, Peter Bull Art Studio, Vanessa Card,
Stuart Carter, Rob Chapman, James Field, Wayne Ford, Chris Forsey,
Mike Foster, Terry Gabbey, Roger Gorringe, Jeremy Gower, Peter
Gregory, Stephen Gyapay, Ron Hayward, Gary Hincks, Sally Holmes,
Richard Hook, Rob Jakeway, John James, Kuo Chen Kang, Aziz Khan,
Stuart Lafford, Ch'en Ling, Steve Lings, Kevin Maddison, Janos
Marffy, Shane Marsh, Rob McCaig, Chris Odgers, Alex Pang, Helen
Parsley, Terry Riley, Andrew Robinson, Chris Rothero, Eric Rowe,
Martin Sanders, Peter Sarson, Mike Saunders, Rob Sheffield, Guy
Smith, Don Simpson, Donato Spedaliere, Nick Spender, Clive
Spong, Stuart Squires, Roger Stewart, Sue Stitt, Ken Stott, Steve
Sweet, Mike Taylor, Alisa Tingley, Catherine Ward, Shane Watson,
Ross Watton, Alison Winfield, John Whetton, Mike White, Stuart
Wilkinson, John Woodcock
Stylists: Jane Coney, Konika Shakar, Thomasina Smith,
Melanie Williams

Previously published as part of a larger compendium, *120 Great
History Projects*.
Picture credits: The Bridgeman Art Library: 28cl; Japan Information
and Cultural Centre; 21t, 28b.

10 9 8 7 6 5 4 3 2 1

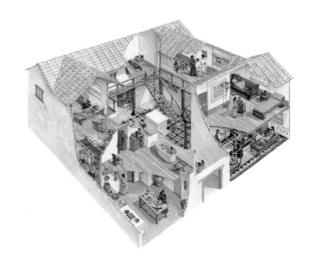

Contents

Early farmers in northern Europe, c. 5000BC

Houses and Homes

Homes provide shelter from the elements first and foremost, but they can be much more than simply a resting place. They can give clues as to what materials were locally available at the time of their construction, and reflect the owner's status and taste. This book investigates a whole host of homes from a variety of different cultures. It takes a look inside to examine some typical features, and recreates some popular dishes of the past.

Different Homes

P eople have always needed to shelter from the weather, and somewhere warm and comfortable to sleep at night. The design of most homes throughout the world depends on the climate. People living in hot countries need their homes to be as cool and airy as possible, while people in cold countries need their homes to be snug and warm. The materials that people use to build their homes usually depend on what they can find around them. Stone, mud, straw and wood are all natural materials that have been used to build homes for thousands of years. By contrast, many modern homes are built from artificial materials such as concrete, steel and glass.

▲ Cool currents

The ancient Greeks built their houses from sun-dried mud bricks laid on stone foundations. The roofs were covered with pottery tiles. Rooms were arranged around an open courtyard so that cool air could build up and circulate through the rooms during the heat of the day.

King of the castle ▶

During the Middle Ages, between 1000 and 1500, castles were built all over Europe, in Scandinavia, Britain, France and Germany, and south to the Mediterranean Sea. They were also built in the Middle East during the Crusades. Castles were built by important people such as kings or queens. They were not only splendid homes that the owners could show off to their friends, but military bases from which the surrounding lands were defended.

◀ Outdoor rooms

The Incas lived in the Andes Mountains in what is now Peru. They built their homes from large blocks of granite, which they quarried from the nearby mountains. The blocks fitted together without mortar. The resulting thick walls provided insulation against the bitter winter cold. A courtyard acted as a large outside room and was used just as much as the inside of the house for everyday living.

Etruscan palace ▶

The Etruscans lived between the Arno and Tiber rivers in western Italy around 2,500 years ago. Wealthy Etruscan families built luxurious palaces decorated with beautiful figurines, bronze statues and engraved mirrors. The Etruscans grew rich by mining copper, tin and iron and trading with the neighboring Greeks and Phoenicians.

◀ Wood and bark

The Iroquois people lived in a densely wooded region of North America. They built their longhouses using a wooden framework covered with sheets of thick bark. The barrel-shaped roofs allowed the rain to run off. These houses were huge because several families lived in each one.

Hunter's home

People have always needed protection from the weather. For most of human history, the Earth's climate has been much colder than it is today. Early humans lived in huts out in the open during summer but moved into caves when the harsh winter weather came. They built stone windbreaks across the entrances. Inside, there were inner huts made of branches and animal bones to provide further protection from the cold. Hunters following herds of game built temporary shelters of branches and leaves in the summer. Families lived in camps of huts made of branches and animal skins. Farther north, where there were no caves and few trees, people built huts from mammoths' leg bones and tusks. Wherever they settled, however, it was very important to be near a supply of fresh water.

▲ **A place to shelter**
At Terra Almata, southern France, hominids (early humans) lived in groups. They established camps made up of several simple shelters, to which they returned year after year. The huts were made of tree branches and weighted down with stones.

YOU WILL NEED

Self-hardening clay, cutting board, modeling tool, twigs, ruler, scissors, card, brown and green acrylic paint, water pot, paintbrushes, white glue and glue brush, fake grass or green fabric.

◀ **Skin huts**
Huts at Monte Verde, Chile, were made of wood covered with animal skins. They are the earliest evidence for human-made shelters in the Americas. The remains were preserved in peaty soil, along with other items, such as a wooden bowl and digging sticks.

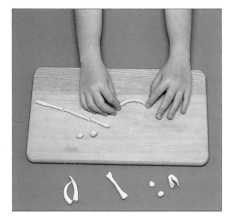

1 Roll out lengths of self-hardening clay, and shape them to look like long and short mammoth bones and tusks. Then make some small clay stones in different sizes.

2 Use the modeling tool to shape the ends of the bones. Then use it to make the stones look uneven. Lay the bones and stones on the cutting board to dry.

3 Lay the twigs next to a ruler. Then use a pair of scissors to cut the twigs so that they are about 6in long. You will need about eight evenly sized twigs in all.

4 Roll out some more clay and spread it unevenly over a piece of card. Paint the clay a brown-green color to look like soil and grass. Do not leave the base to dry.

5 Push the twigs into the clay base, and arch them over to form a cone-shaped frame. Glue a few stones onto the clay at the base of each of the twigs.

6 Cover the twigs with pieces of fake grass or green fabric. Leave a gap at one side for the entrance. Glue the pieces in place. Take care not to cover up the stones around the base.

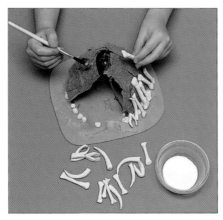

7 Neatly glue the long mammoth bones and tusks all over the outside of the hunter's shelter. Fill in any gaps with smaller bones. Leave the hunter's home to dry.

When wood was scarce, the heavy bones of an elephant-like animal called a mammoth were used to weigh down the grass and animal hides that covered the hunter's shelter.

Mud-brick house

The great cities of ancient Egypt were built along the banks of the River Nile. Small towns grew up haphazardly around them. Special workers' towns, such as Deir el-Medina, were also set up around major burial sites and temples to be close to the building work.

Mud brick was used for most buildings, from royal palaces to workers' dwellings. Only temples and pyramids were built to last – they were made from stone. Most homes had roofs supported with palm logs and floors of packed earth. In the evenings, people would sit on the flat roofs or walk in the cool, shady gardens.

▲ Tomb workers
The village of Deir el-Medina housed the skilled workers who built the royal tombs in the Valley of the Kings. The men were required to work for eight days out of ten.

clay

▲ Mud brick
The Egyptians dried bricks in the sun using the thick clay soil left behind by the Nile floods. The clay was taken to a brick yard and mixed with water, pebbles and chopped straw.

Templates

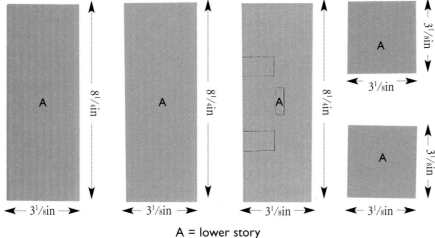

A = lower story

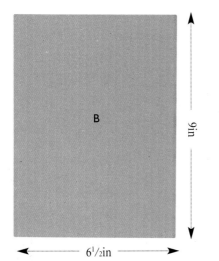

B = base

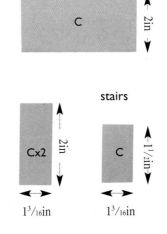

stairs

C = upper story

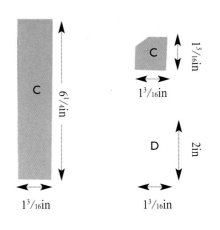

D = sunshade roof

YOU WILL NEED

Thick card, 1⅝ x 1³⁄₁₆in thin card (for stairs), pencil, ruler, scissors, white glue and glue brush, masking tape, balsa wood, plaster of Paris, water pot and brush, acrylic paint (green, white, yellow and red), paintbrush, sandpaper, straw.

1 Use the templates to measure and cut out the pieces for the house. Glue together the baseboard, walls and ceiling of the lower story. Reinforce the joints with masking tape.

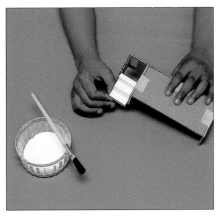

2 Glue together the roof and walls of the top story. Fold the thin card as shown for the stairs, and glue into place. Tape joints to reinforce. Glue the top story to the lower story.

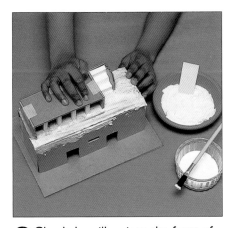

3 Glue balsa pillars into the front of the top story. When the house is dry, cover it in a wet paste of plaster of Paris. Paint the pillars red or another color of your choice.

4 Paint your model the same color as dried mud. Next paint a green strip along the wall. Use the masking tape to ensure the edges are straight. Sand any rough edges.

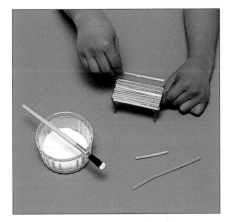

5 Now make a shelter for the rooftop. Use four balsa struts as supports. Glue the piece of card (D) and cover it with pieces of straw. Glue the shelter into place.

Mediterranean Sea

Giza
Saqqara Dashur
Meidum

Western
desert

Red
Sea

River
Nile

Eastern
desert

▲ Living by the river

Egyptians built their homes along the banks of the River Nile. Many pyramids, such as those at Giza, are found here, too.

Egyptian houses had a large main room that opened directly into the street. In many homes, stairs led up to the roof. People slept there during hot weather.

Roman house

Only the wealthiest Romans could afford to live in a private house. The front door opened onto a short passage leading to the *atrium*, a central court or entrance hall. Front rooms on either side of the passage were usually bedrooms. Sometimes, though, they were used as workshops or shops and had shutters that opened out to the street.

The center of the atrium was open to the sky. Below this opening was a small pool to collect rainwater. If you were a guest or had business, you would be shown into the office, or *tablinium*. The dining room, or *triclinium,* was often the grandest room of all. Extremely wealthy Romans also had a summer dining room, which looked out onto the garden.

▲ **House and garden**
The outside of a Roman town house was usually very plain, but inside it was decorated with colorful wall paintings and intricate mosaics.

Templates

Cut out the pieces of card following the measurements shown.

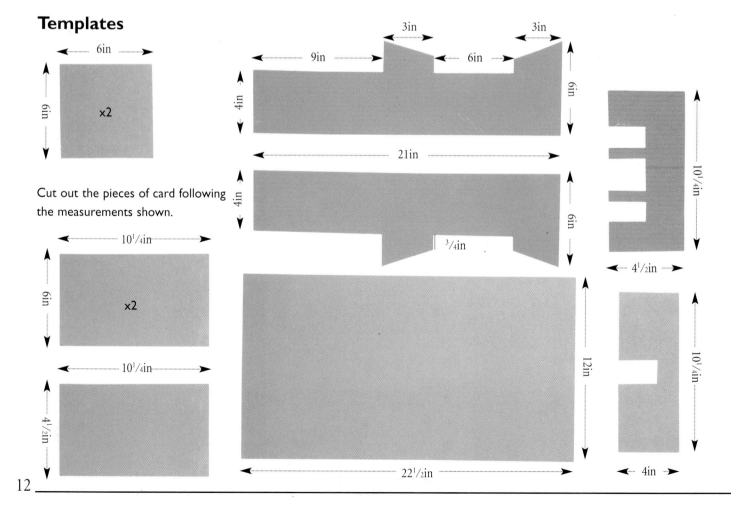

YOU WILL NEED

Pencil, ruler, thick card, scissors, white glue and glue brush, masking tape, corrugated card, acrylic paints, paintbrushes, water pot, thin card.

ivy

rose

▲ **Garden delights**

Trailing ivy and sweet-smelling roses often grew in the beautiful walled gardens of a Roman house.

I When you have cut out all the templates, edge each piece with glue. Press the templates together and reinforce with masking tape as shown. These form the walls of your house.

2 Measure your model and cut out pieces of corrugated card for the roof sections. Stick them together with glue as shown above. Paint all of the roofs with red paint.

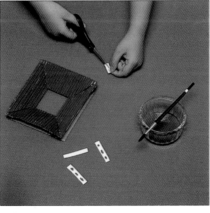

3 Rainwater running down the roof above the atrium was directed into a pool by gutters and water spouts. Make gutters from strips of thin card and pierce holes for the spouts.

4 Paint the walls of the house, using masking tape to get a straight line. Glue on the roof sections. You could then cover the walls of the house with some authentic Roman graffiti.

Roman houses had high, windowless walls to keep out the sun, making them cool and shady inside. High ceilings and wide doors made the most of the light from the open atrium and garden. Houses were made from whatever building materials were available and included stone, mud bricks, cement and timber. Clay tiles usually covered the roof.

Celtic roundhouse

It was dark and smoky inside a Celtic roundhouse but quite cosy and comfortable. A thatched roof kept the house warm in the winter but cool in the summer. Houses were heated by a wood or peat fire burning in a pit in the center of the room. The hearth was the heart of the home, and the fire was kept burning day and night, all year around. Smoke from the fire escaped through the thatch.

straw

YOU WILL NEED

String, ruler, felt-tipped pen, brown card, scissors, two pieces of stiff white card (31in x 4½in), white glue and glue brush, masking tape, non-hardening modeling material, rolling pin, straw, corrugated card, seven pieces of 18in-long doweling, bradawl.

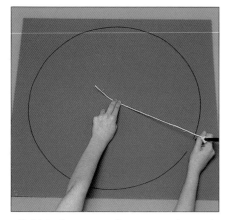

1 Use the piece of string, a ruler and a felt-tipped pen to draw a circle with a radius of 10in on the brown card. Carefully cut out the circle using a pair of scissors.

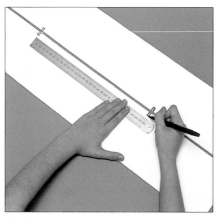

2 Draw a mark every 12in along the edges of the two pieces of white card. Cut into each mark to make a notch. Glue the two pieces of card together at one end.

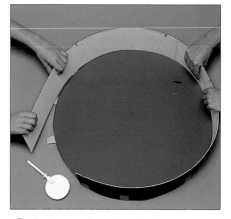

3 Fit the card wall to the base of your house, making sure that the notches are along the top. Glue the wall in place and secure it with masking tape.

4 Roll out the modeling material into sections 5in wide. Sprinkle straw onto the modeling material and roll it into the surface. Make enough sections to cover the card wall.

5 Firmly press each modeling material section onto the card wall until the whole wall is covered. Remember to leave a space where the notches are at the top of the wall.

6 Cut a large circle with a diameter of 3ft from the corrugated card. Cut a small circle in the center. Cut the large circle into sections 22in wide along the edge.

7 Glue pieces of straw onto each piece of card. These will form the roof sections. Start on the outside edge and work your way in toward the center. Use three layers of straw.

8 Wrap two pieces of masking tape ½in apart around the middle of six lengths of doweling. Tie string between the pieces of tape. Allow a 5in length of string between each stick.

9 Place one length of doweling in the middle of the base. Secure it with modeling material. Place the tied sticks over the base as shown above. Lodge the sticks into the wall notches.

10 Fix the sticks in place in the wall notches using modeling material. Cover with an extra piece. Tie the top of the sticks to the upright stick using more string.

11 Tie together the ends of the string between the last two sticks that make up the roof section. Remember to keep the string taut to stop the roof from collapsing.

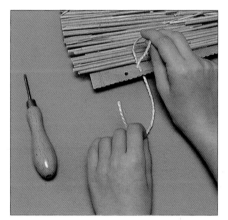

12 Use the bradawl to pierce two holes on both edges at the top and bottom of each straw roof section. Carefully thread a piece of string through each hole.

13 Use the ends of the string to tie the straw roof sections firmly onto the roof structure. Carry on adding the straw sections until the roof is completely covered.

Most houses had no windows. The only light came through the open door. Doorways were low and protected by a porch to keep out the wind and rain.

Native American tepee

Many Native American tribes, such as the Cheyenne of the Great Plains, were nomadic. Their life was dependent on the movement of buffalo. The animals supplied the tribe with food, clothing and shelter. Many tribes lived in tepees, which were easy to build and also easy to pack up when it was time to move on.

Your tepee is a simple version of a Plains tepee. These were large, heavy shelters made from stretched and tanned buffalo skin.

YOU WILL NEED

An old double sheet (measuring around 100 x 31in) cut into a semicircle with a diameter of 60in, scissors, pencil, tape measure, large and small paintbrushes, acrylic paints, water pot, string, 12 bamboo sticks, three small sticks, large stones.

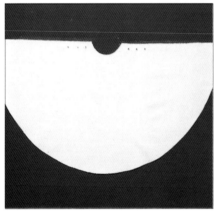

1 Cut out a smaller semicircle 18in across and 8in deep as shown. Make three evenly spaced holes either side of this semicircle. Start 2½in from the center and 1³⁄₁₆in from the flat edge.

2 Using a pencil and tape measure, draw out a pattern of triangles, lines and circles on the sheet. Make the pattern bold and simple, similar to the one shown. Paint it and leave it to dry.

3 Tie three bamboo sticks together at one end and arrange them on the ground to form a tripod. Lean the remaining bamboo sticks against the tripod. Leave a gap for the entrance.

4 Now take the painted sheet (your tepee cover) and wrap it over the bamboo frame. Overlap the two sides at the top of the frame so that the holes you made earlier join up.

5 Insert a small stick through the two top holes to join them. Do this for each of the other holes. You can place stones around the bottom of the sheet to secure your tepee.

Arctic igloo

In the Inuit language, the word *iglu* was actually used to describe any type of house. A shelter such as the one you can build below was called an *igluigaq*. Most Inuit igloos were simple, dome-like structures, which were used as shelters during the winter hunting trips. A small entrance tunnel prevented cold winds from entering the igloo and trapped warm air inside. Outside, the temperature could be as low as −158°F. Inside, heat from the stove, candles and the warmth of the hunter's body kept the air at around 41°F.

YOU WILL NEED

Self-hardening clay, cutting board, rolling pin, ruler, modeling tool, scissors, thick card (8 x 8in), pair of compasses, pencil, water pot, white paint, paintbrush.

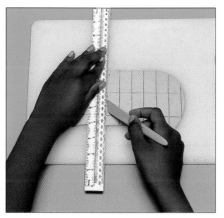

1 Roll out the self-hardening clay. It should be ⁵⁄₁₆in thick. Cut out 30 blocks of clay. Twenty-four of the blocks must be 1½ x ¾in and the other six blocks must be ¾ x ½in.

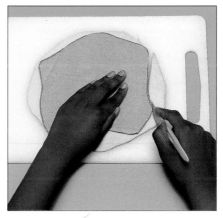

2 Cut out some card to make an irregular base shape. Roll out more clay (⁵⁄₁₆in thick). Put the template on the clay and cut around it to make the base of the igloo.

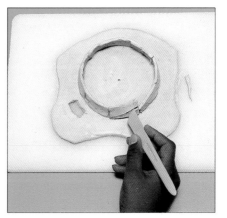

3 Mark a circle (diameter 4½in) on the base. Cut out a rectangle on the edge of the circle (¾ x 1½in). Stick nine large blocks around the circle using water. Cut across two blocks as shown.

4 Using your modeling tool, carefully cut a small piece of clay from the corner of each of the remaining blocks of clay as shown above. Discard the pieces of cut clay.

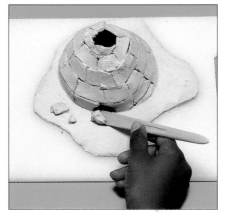

5 Build up the igloo dome, slanting each block in as you go. Use the six small blocks at the top and leave a gap. Form an entrance behind the rectangle cut into the base. Then paint it white.

Inuit hunters made temporary shelters by fitting ice blocks together to form a spiraling, dome-shaped igloo. Only firmly packed snow was used to make the ice blocks.

Medieval castle

In the Middle Ages, castles were built as fortified homes for wealthy lords. The castle needed to be big enough for the lord's family, servants and private army, and strong enough to withstand attack. The outer walls were very high to prevent attackers from climbing over them.

Building a castle ▶
Hundreds of workers were needed to build a castle. Raw materials, such as stone, timber and iron had to be transported to the site, often over great distances.

Templates

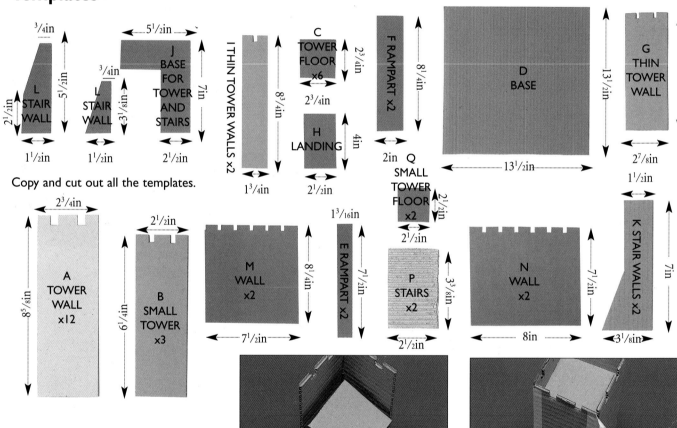

Copy and cut out all the templates.

YOU WILL NEED

Ruler, pencil, scissors, four sheets of 34 x 22in thick card, 7½ x 2¾in sheet of thin card, 20 x 6in sheet of corrugated card, white glue and glue brush, masking tape, pair of compasses, acrylic paints, paintbrush, water pot.

1 Cut the stairs from the corrugated card, thin tower wall (G) from thin card and the rest from thick card. Glue two A walls onto tower floor C. Glue upper floor C in place.

2 Glue the open edges of the floor, tower base and standing wall and stick the other two walls in place. Tape strips of masking tape over all the outside corners of the tower walls.

3 Draw a 3¾in-diameter circle on thick card. Mark it into quarters. Cut out two quarters for the thin tower floors. Glue the two right-angled walls I and the floors into position.

4 Glue the edges of the thin tower walls I. Curve thin card wall section G and stick it onto the right-angled walls. Strengthen the joins with masking tape. Glue tower on base D.

5 Glue the other towers at each corner of the castle base. Glue the bottom and side edges of the walls M and N and stick them between the towers. Glue ramparts E and F to the walls as shown.

6 Make the small tower B in just the same way as you have made all the other towers. Put two of the walls in place, then the floors and finally the third wall.

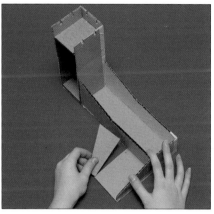

7 Glue the small tower at the end of the longer arm of the castle's stair base section J. Glue the two long stair walls K and each stair wall L into place as shown above.

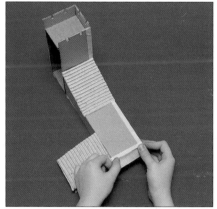

8 Glue landing H onto the straight edges of the stair walls. Stick stairs P onto the sloped edges. Secure with tape. Then stick the whole structure to one side wall of the castle.

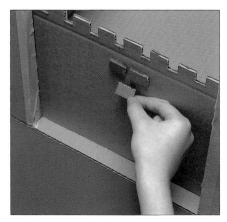

9 Cut out some pieces of thick card and glue them to the walls of your castle and stair-tower. When you have finished, paint the castle to look like stone and paint in some windows.

The walls of a real stone castle were up to 16ft thick and built of individual stones painstakingly cemented together.

Inside the Home

▲ Elaborate patterns
The Native American tribes of southwestern North America were renowned for their beautiful pottery. Each tribe used geometric designs and bright colors to decorate household objects such as this striking tankard.

U*nless they happened to be very rich, most people throughout history have lived in simple but extremely functional homes. Most families had few pieces of furniture or other household items. Their homes consisted of one large room, which was used for a number of different activities, such as cooking, eating and sleeping. By contrast, modern homes are arranged so that separate rooms are used for specific activities, and each room is furnished for that purpose.*

▲ Spacious layout
The rooms of a Chinese house from the Han Dynasty (206BC–AD220) were built around a courtyard and small garden. Family rooms were separate from the main reception area, which was used for entertaining.

▲ Greek vase
This Greek vase is in the Geometric Style, dating from between 1000BC and 700BC. The detailed pattern took a long time to create so it was very expensive to buy. The vase would have been used only for special occasions.

Lasting tradition ▶

Many modern lifestyles have not changed much over the centuries. The Japanese have long favored simple interior spaces divided by light partitions instead of solid walls. Traditional paper windows have been replaced by glass, which captures the effect of paper.

◀ All in one

Huts made from stone, turf and animal bones were built by the Thule people of the Arctic. The main feature of the inside of the hut was a fire. Animal skins were draped on the walls and floor to give insulation against the bitter cold.

House and garden ▶

Wealthy Japanese nobles lived in huge *shinden* (single-story homes) with many different rooms. The various members of the noble family, and their servants, lived in different parts of the shinden. Streams flowed from the garden through the rooms of the house.

Egyptian tiles

The ancient Egyptians loved to decorate their surroundings. Wealthy citizens had the walls of their homes plastered and painted in bright colors. The rooms of their houses included bedrooms, living rooms, kitchens in thatched courtyards and workshops. Homes were furnished with beds, chairs, stools and benches. Many beautiful tiles have been found in the tombs of the pharaohs, and it is thought that they were used to decorate the furniture and floors of their magnificent palaces.

1 Copy the two tile shapes, about 5cm deep, on one sheet of card. Cut them out. Draw around them on the other sheet to make the whole pattern. Trim the edge as in step 2.

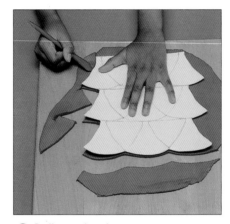

2 Roll out the clay onto a cutting board with a rolling pin. Place the overall outline over the clay and carefully trim the edges using the modeling tool. Discard the extra clay.

3 Mark the individual tile patterns onto the clay. Cut through the lines but do not separate them fully. Score patterns of leaves and flowers onto the surface of the clay. Separate each tile.

4 When one side of each tile has dried, turn the tile over and leave the other side to dry. When the tiles are fully dry, use a piece of sandpaper to smooth off the edges.

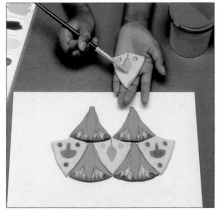

5 The tiles are now ready to paint. Use bright colors to paint over the patterns you made earlier. When you have finished, leave the tiles to dry in a warm place.

The tiles you have made are similar to ones found at a royal palace in Thebes, the capital city of ancient Egypt. The design looks rather like a lotus, the sacred flower of ancient Egypt.

Greek dolphin fresco

Frescoes – paintings on plaster – were a popular way of decorating the walls of palaces on the Greek island of Crete. To make the frescoes last as long as possible, they were painted directly onto wet plaster. Most Greek frescoes show scenes from palace life and the natural world. The paintings are a vital source of information for modern historians. A large fresco decorated the walls of the queen's apartments in a magnificent palace at Knossos. The fresco shows lively dolphins and fish swimming underwater.

YOU WILL NEED

Pencil, sheet of white paper
(8 x 7in), rolling pin,
self-hardening clay, cutting board,
rolling pin, modeling tool, ruler,
pin, sandpaper, acrylic paints,
paintbrush, water pot.

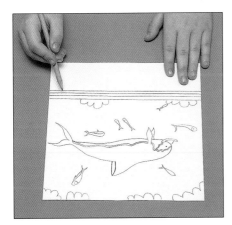

1 Draw a picture of a dolphin onto the sheet of white paper. Add some smaller fish and some seaweed for decoration. Refer to the final picture as a guide for your drawing.

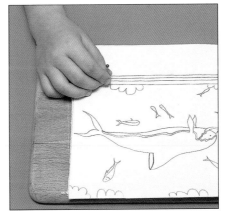

2 Roll out some clay. Tidy up the edges using the modeling tool and ruler. Place your picture over the clay and use a pin to prick holes through the outline onto the clay below.

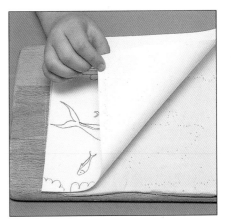

3 Peel the paper off to reveal your picture marked out in dots. Leave the base to dry completely. Then sand it down with fine sandpaper for a smooth finish.

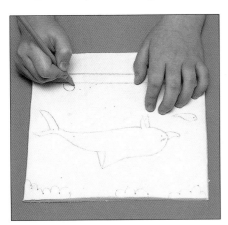

4 Use your pencil to join up the dots on the surface of the clay. Do not press too hard on the clay. When you have finished, you will have a replica of your original drawing.

5 You can then begin to paint the picture. When you have finished, paint in two stripes at the bottom of the picture. These indicate where the fresco would have ended on the wall.

Today, the frescoes at Knossos are copies based on fragments of the original pictures. They are a valuable source of information about Minoan customs.

Roman mosaic

The Romans loved to decorate their homes, and the floors of some wealthy houses were covered with mosaic pictures. These pictures might show hunting scenes, the harvest or Roman gods. They were made by using *tesserae* – cubes of stone, pottery or glass – which were pressed into soft cement. Making a mosaic was rather like doing a jigsaw puzzle.

tesserae

Tiny tiles ▲

The floor of a room in an average Roman town house may have been made up of over 100,000 tesserae.

YOU WILL NEED

Paper, pencil, ruler, scissors, large sheet of card, self-hardening clay, rolling pin, cutting board, modeling tool, acrylic paints, paintbrush, water pot, clear varnish and brush (optional), plaster paste, spreader, muslin rag.

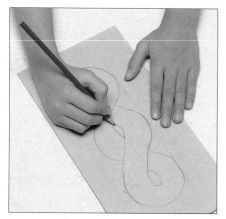

1 Sketch your design onto a rough sheet of paper. A simple design is always easier to work with. Cut the sheet of card to measure 10 x 4in. Copy your design onto it.

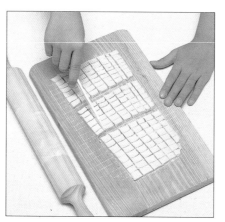

2 Roll out the clay on the cutting board. Use a ruler to measure out small squares (your tiles) on the clay. Cut out the tiles using the modeling tool and then leave them to dry.

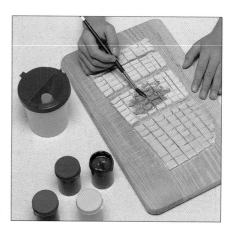

3 Paint the dry tiles different colors as shown above. When the paint is dry, you can give the tiles a coat of varnish for extra strength and shine. Leave the tiles to dry completely.

4 Spread plaster paste onto the sheet of card, a small part at a time. While the paste is still wet, press in your tiles, following your design. Use the rough sketch as an extra guide.

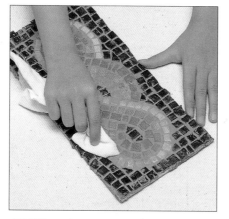

5 When the mosaic is dry, use a muslin rag to polish the surface of the tiles. Any other soft, dry rag will do. When you have finished, you can display your mosaic in your house.

Mosaics were displayed in dining rooms and courtyards where visitors would see them.

Roman kitchen

The kitchens of wealthy Romans were equipped with all kinds of bronze pots, pans, strainers and ladles. Pottery storage jars held wine, olive oil and sauces. Herbs, vegetables and joints of meat hung from hooks in the roof. There were no cans, and no fridges or freezers to keep the food fresh. Instead, food had to be preserved in oil or by drying, smoking, salting or pickling. Food was boiled, fried, grilled and stewed. Larger kitchens might include stone ovens for baking bread or spits for roasting meat.

YOU WILL NEED

Ruler, pencil, thick card, scissors, white glue and glue brush, masking tape, acrylic paints, paintbrush, water pot, red felt-tipped pen, plaster paste, sandpaper, balsa wood, self-hardening clay, cutting board, modeling tool.

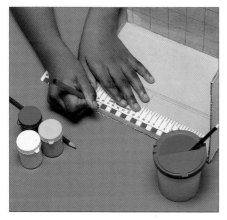

1 Glue pieces of card to make the walls and floor. Secure with masking tape. Paint the floor gray and pencil in stone tiles. Paint the walls yellow and blue. Draw on stripes with the red pen.

2 Use some card to make a stove and coat it with plaster paste. When it is dry, rub it smooth with sandpaper. Make a grate from two strips of card and four bits of balsa wood, glued together.

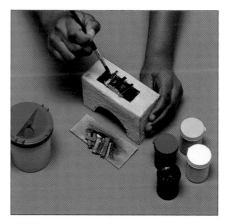

3 Use some acrylic paints to color the stove as shown above. Use small pieces of balsa wood to make a pile of wood fuel to store underneath the stove.

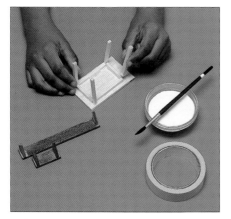

4 Make a table and shelves from pieces of balsa wood as shown above. Glue them together and secure the joins with masking tape. Leave them to dry before painting them brown.

5 Use a piece of clay to model pots, pans, bowls, storage jars, perhaps even a frying pan or an egg poacher. Leave the utensils to dry before painting them a suitable color.

Foods in a Roman kitchen were stored in baskets, bowls or sacks. Wine, oil and sauces were stored in pottery jars called *amphorae*.

Chinese lantern

Chinese festivals are linked to agricultural seasons. The festivals include celebrations of sowing and harvest, dances, horse racing and the eating of specially prepared foods. The Chinese festival best known around the world today is the New Year or Spring Festival. Its date falls on the first full moon between January 21 and February 19. At the end of the Chinese New Year, dumplings made of rice flour are prepared for the Lantern Festival. This festival began during the Tang Dynasty or "Golden Age" (AD618–906) – a time when the arts prospered, new trade routes opened in foreign lands and boundaries expanded as a result of successful military campaigns.

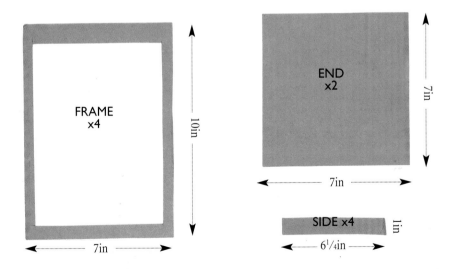

▲ Bright lights

During the Lantern Festival, lanterns are hung outside the house to represent the first full moon of the Chinese New Year. Lanterns were once made from silk or glass and decorated with ornate images or calligraphy (handwriting).

Templates

FRAME
x4

7in

10in

END
x2

7in

7in

SIDE x4

6¼in

1in

▲ Fire power

You could decorate your lantern with a firework display. The Chinese invented gunpowder in the AD700s. It was first used to make fireworks in the 900s.

Using the measurements above, draw the ten templates onto thick card (the templates are not drawn to scale). Cut them out carefully using a pair of scissors.

YOU WILL NEED

Thick card, pencil, ruler, scissors, pair of compasses, white glue and glue brush, red tissue paper, blue acrylic paint, paintbrush, water pot, thin blue and yellow card, wire, masking tape, bamboo stick, small torch, fringing fabric.

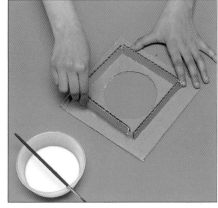

1 Using a pair of compasses, draw a 3⅛in-diameter circle in the middle of one of the end pieces. Cut out the circle using the scissors. Glue on the four sides.

2 Glue together the four frame pieces. Then glue both end pieces onto the frame. When it is dry, cover the frame with red tissue paper. Glue one side at a time.

3 Paint the top of the lantern blue. Cut the borders out of blue card. Glue to the top and bottom of the frame. Stick a thin strip of yellow card to the bottom to make a border.

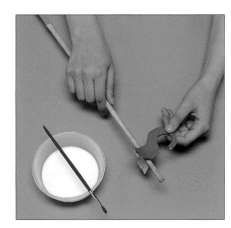
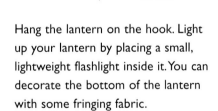

Hang the lantern on the hook. Light up your lantern by placing a small, lightweight flashlight inside it. You can decorate the bottom of the lantern with some fringing fabric.

4 Make two small holes opposite each other at the top of the lantern as shown above. Pass the ends of a loop of wire through the holes. Tape the ends to secure the wire.

5 Make a hook from thick card. Split the ends opposite the hook as shown above. Wrap the ends around the bamboo stick and glue them together, securing with masking tape.

Japanese paper screen

Builders faced many challenges when they designed homes in ancient Japan. Not only did buildings have to provide shelter against extremes of climate, they also had to withstand earthquakes. Lightweight, single-story houses were made of straw, paper and wood. These would bend and sway in an earthquake. If they did collapse, or were swept away by floods, they would be less likely than a stone building to injure the people inside.

Japanese buildings were designed as a series of box-like rooms. A one-room hut was sufficient for a farming family. Dividing screens and partitions could be moved around to suit people's needs. Many houses had verandas (open platforms) beneath overhanging eaves. People could sit here taking in the fresh air, keeping lookout or enjoying the view.

paper

wood

▲ Screened off

Wood and paper were used to make screens for both the outer and inner walls of many Japanese homes. The screens were pushed back to provide peaceful garden views and welcome cool breezes during the hot summer.

▲ Fine work

Folding screens became decorative items as well as providing privacy and protection from drafts. This panel was made during the Edo period (1603–1868), when crafts flourished.

Simple living ▶

Modern rural Japanese homes are built in the same way and using similar materials to those of ancient Japan. Screens and sliding walls can be moved to block drafts and for privacy. Straw and rush mats, called *tatami*, cover the floor.

YOU WILL NEED

Gold paper (19 x 17½in), pencil, ruler, scissors, thick card (19 x 8¾in), craft knife, cutting board, white glue and glue brush, fabric paints, paintbrush, water pot, fabric tape.

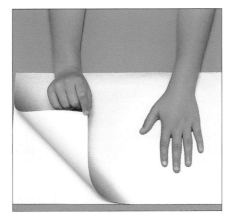

1 Cut two pieces of gold paper to measure 19 x 8¾in. Use a craft knife to cut out a piece of card the same size. Stick the gold paper to each side of the card.

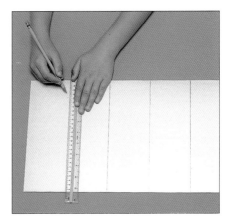

2 When the glue has dried, use a ruler and pencil to mark out six panels of equal size on one side of the gold-covered card. Each panel should measure 8¾ x 3⅛in.

3 Now turn the card over. Paint a traditional picture of Japanese irises in shades of blue and green fabric paint as shown above. Leave the paint to dry.

4 Turn the screen over so the plain, unpainted side is facing you. Using scissors or a craft knife, carefully cut out each panel along the lines that you marked earlier.

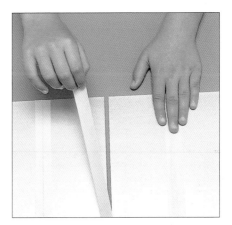

5 Now use fabric tape to join each of your panels together, leaving a small gap between each panel. The tape will act as a hinge for each section of your Japanese screen.

Irises are a popular image in Japanese homes. The pretty blue flowers are a symbol of absent friends.

Native American tankard

The Native Americans were skilled craftspeople. Most tribes wove baskets and blankets from plant fibers. Some baskets were coiled so tightly that they could hold water. The tribes of the Southwest were renowned for their pottery. The Apache tribe made black and white bowls that became known as burial pots. This was because they were broken when their owner died and buried with the body. Archaeologists have also found beautiful pots dating back to around 1000BC.

> ### YOU WILL NEED
> Self-hardening clay, cutting board, rolling board, water pot, pencil, selection of acrylic or poster paints, selection of paintbrushes, nontoxic varnish.

1 Roll out a slab of clay into a flat circle about 4in across. Roll two sausage shapes. Dampen the perimeter of the circle and then stick one end of the sausage to it as shown above.

2 Coil the sausage around. When the first sausage runs out, use the other clay sausage. Use your damp fingers to smooth the coils into a tankard shape and smooth the outside.

3 Roll out another small sausage shape of clay to make the handle of the tankard. Dampen the ends and press it onto the clay pot to make a handle shape. Leave it to dry.

4 Using a sharp pencil, mark out a striking design on your tankard. You can follow the traditional Indian design shown here, or you could make up one of your own.

5 Using poster paints or acrylic paints, color in the pattern. Use a fine brush for tiny checked patterns and thin lines. When it is dry, coat the mug with one or two layers of varnish.

Each tribe had its unique designs and used certain colors. The geometric patterns on the tankard above were common to tribes of the Southwest.

Viking drinking horn

The Viking sagas (long stories) tell of many drunken celebrations. They helped relieve the strain of the long, dark winters. Warriors would have toasted each other with beer or mead (an alcoholic drink made by fermenting honey). They drank from drinking horns made from the horns of cattle. Unless a drinking horn was being passed around a number of people, it could not be put down and the contents had to be consumed in one go. Drink was ladled out from giant barrels and tubs.

YOU WILL NEED

Thick paper, pencil, ruler, scissors, mug, masking tape, brown paper, self-hardening clay, newspaper, water pot, acrylic paints, paintbrush, silver paper, white glue and glue brush.

1 Cut the thick paper into 11in-long strips all with different widths. Roll the widest strip into a ring using the rim of a mug as a guide. Secure the paper ring with masking tape.

2 Roll up the next widest strip, and secure it with masking tape. Place the small ring inside the large ring and fix with tape. Make more rings, each one a bit smaller than the one before.

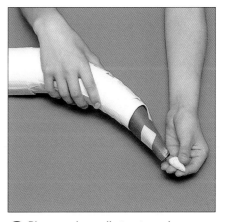

3 Place each small ring into the next largest, binding with tape to make a tapered horn. Roll brown paper into a cone to make a point and bind it in position. Round off the end with clay.

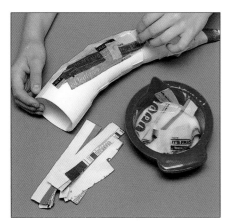

4 Cover the horn with papier-mâché. Cut strips of newspaper, soak them in water and glue them to the horn. Leave to dry and then add more layers of papier-mâché. Leave to dry again.

5 When dry, paint the horn white, giving it a black or brown tip. Cut the silver paper into a pattern and glue it to the rim of the horn. Viking horns were often decorated with silver.

Drinking horns were used on special occasions such as festivals and victory celebrations.

31

Arctic oil lamp

The Arctic is one of the wildest, harshest, environments on Earth. Arctic winters are long, dark and bitterly cold. A thick layer of snow and ice blankets the region for much of the year. A fire was the main feature of an Arctic home. In Inuit shelters, seal or whale blubber were burned in stone lamps to provide light and additional heat. With fires and lamps burning, the shelters could be surprisingly warm and bright.

▲ Underground houses

Ancient Arctic peoples built their houses under the ground to protect them from the freezing conditions above. Often, the walls and floor were lined with animal skins to provide extra insulation against the cold.

▲ Colony in the cold

When Viking warrior Erik the Red landed in Greenland in AD983, he and his men built houses of turf and stone. These shelters provided excellent insulation against the cold.

A harsh climate ▶

The Arctic lies at the far north of our planet within the Arctic Circle. Much of the Arctic is a vast, frozen ocean, surrounded by the northernmost parts of Asia, Europe, North America and Greenland. The Arctic is characterized by low temperatures, often as low as −158°F in the winter. For anyone living in the region, it is vital to keep as warm as possible. Homes may be buried underground, with an entrance through the roof.

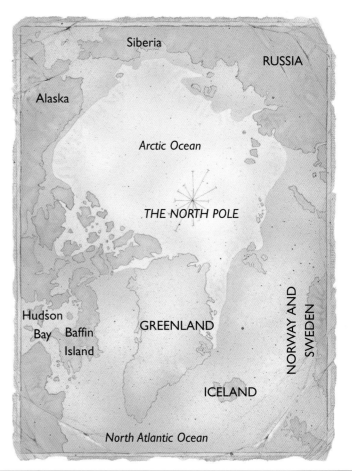

YOU WILL NEED

Self-hardening clay, rolling pin, cutting board, ruler, pair of compasses, sharp pencil, modeling tool, water pot, dark gray and light gray paint, small paintbrush.

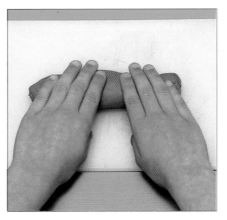

1 Roll out a piece of clay. Draw out a circle with a radius of 2in, and cut the circle out using the modeling tool. Roll more clay out into a long sausage shape 1ft long and ¾in thick.

2 Wet the edge of the clay circle and stick the sausage shape around it. Use the rounded end of the modeling tool to blend the edges firmly into the base.

3 Use your modeling tool to cut a small triangular notch at the edge of the circle. This will make a small lip for the front of your oil lamp.

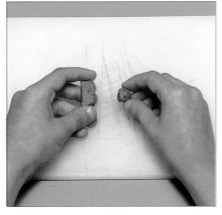

4 Shape a piece of clay into a small head. Use another piece to shape some shoulders. Stick the head to the shoulders by wetting the clay and holding the pieces firmly together.

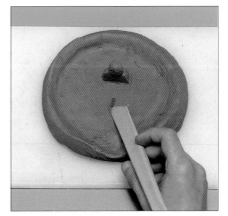

5 Stick the small figure just off center on the base of the oil lamp. Then use the modeling tool to make a small groove on the base. This is for holding the oil.

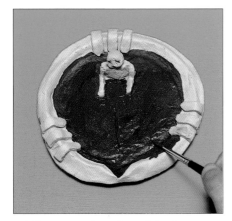

6 Decorate the edge of the lamp with extra pieces of clay. Once dry, paint the lamp using dark gray and light gray paint. _Safety note: do not attempt to burn anything in your lamp._

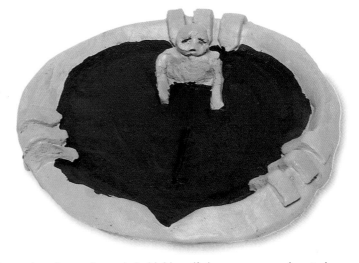

Stone lamps burning seal or whale blubber (fat) cast a warm glow in homes throughout the Arctic region. A lighted wick of moss or animal fur was placed in a bowl filled with fat, and the lamp was left to burn slowly.

Food and Feasts

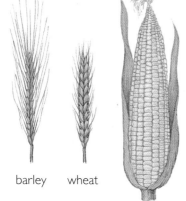

barley   wheat

corn

squashes

▲ Fruits of the soil

The first plants to be cultivated already grew in the wild. For example, wheat and barley were grown from wild plants in the Middle East. Corn, squashes and beans were the first to be grown in Central America.

A great change in human history took place around 10,000BC. Instead of gathering the seeds of wild plants, people began to grow their own food. They selected and sowed seeds from the healthiest plants to produce crops to harvest for food. People also began to breed cattle, goats and sheep for meat and milk. Different traditions surrounding the preparation, cooking and eating of food developed. Food was a way of showing hospitality to family and strangers. Some foods were given a religious meaning and came to be used for special festivals.

◄ Back-breaking work

Early farmers gathered grain from edible wild grasses and then planted seeds from the plants for the following year's harvest. They had only simple tools and the crops were harvested using wooden sickles set with sharp flint blades.

▲ Jobs for the family

Farmers on this settlement in Germany are thatching the roof of a longhouse. The women are grinding grain between stones to make bread. They will add water to the flour and shape the dough into flat loaves, which will be baked in a clay oven.

▲ A farming village

The farmers of this village in southern England have built round, thatched houses next to their wheat fields. They also keep domesticated cattle for milk, meat and skins. Every morning the cattle were led from the village to pastures outside.

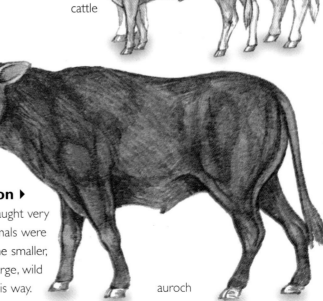

cattle

Domestication ▶

When people changed from hunting to farming, they caught very young animals to raise by hand. Larger, more aggressive animals were killed. Gradually, new domesticated strains evolved from the smaller, more docile animals. Domestic cattle were bred from large, wild animals called aurochs in this way.

auroch

Stone Age food

The hunter-gatherers of the Stone Age had a varied diet. Gradually, they learned that they could eat certain plants and got to know where and when they could find them. From spring to fall, women and children foraged for berries, nuts, eggs, and the roots, shoots and leaves of vegetables. In summer, fruits and plant seeds were picked and stored to eat later.

dandelion leaves

woodland fungus

◄ Foraging for food

The food that prehistoric people ate came mostly from plants. Woodlands in fall were a rich source of food, with plenty of fruits, fungi and nuts.

YOU WILL NEED

A large saucepan, 1¼lb blueberries, 1¼lb blackberries, wooden spoon, 7oz whole hazelnuts, honeycomb, tablespoon, ladle, serving bowl.

1 Choose fruit that is fresh and firm. Wash your hands before you start, and ask an adult to help you cook. Wash the blueberries and pour them into the large saucepan.

2 Next wash the blackberries and pour them into the pan with the blueberries. Use a wooden spoon to stir the fruits gently without crushing them.

3 Take the whole hazelnuts and pour them into the pan with the blueberries and blackberries. Carefully stir the contents until the fruits and nuts are thoroughly mixed.

4 Add six tablespoons of honey from the honeycomb. (You could use honey from a jar instead.) Then ask an adult to help you cook the mixture, gradually bringing it to the boil.

5 Simmer the fruit and nut mixture for about 20 minutes. Take the pan off the stove and leave it to cool. Use a ladle to transfer your dessert into a serving bowl.

In prehistoric times, people cooked fruit in this way to preserve it as jam. Clay pots were used for cooking and storing the jam.

Egyptian pastries

People in ancient Egypt were often given food as payment for their work. Foods such as bread, onions and salted fish were washed down with sweet, grainy beer. Flour was often gritty, and the teeth of many mummified bodies show signs of severe wear and tear. An Egyptian meal could be finished off with nuts, such as almonds, or sweet fruits, such as figs and dates.

onions

◀ **Fruits and vegetables**

Onions, leeks, cabbages, melons, grapes and many other fruits and vegetables were grown in ancient Egypt.

YOU WILL NEED
Mixing bowl, wooden spoon, 7oz stoneground flour, ½ tsp salt, 1 tsp baking powder, 3oz chopped butter, 2¼oz honey, 3 tbsp milk, floured surface, caraway seeds, baking tray.

1 Mix the flour, salt and baking powder in the bowl. Add the chopped butter. Using your fingers, rub the butter into the mixture until it resembles fine breadcrumbs.

2 Add 1½oz of honey and combine it with the mixture. Stir in the milk to form a stiff dough. Shape the dough into a ball and place it on a floured board or work surface.

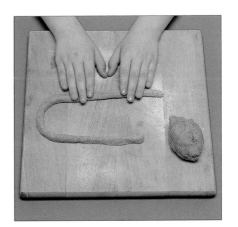

3 Divide the dough into three. Roll each piece into long strips as shown above. Take each strip and coil it into a spiral to make a cake. Make two other cakes in the same way.

4 Now sprinkle each spiral cake with caraway seeds and place them onto a greased baking tray. Finish off by glazing the cakes with the remainder of the honey.

5 Ask an adult to bake the cakes in an oven at 350°F/Gas Mark 4 for approximately 20 minutes. When they are ready, take the cakes out and leave them to cool.

Egyptian pastries were often shaped in spirals. Other popular shapes were rings like doughnuts. The Egyptians did not have sugar, so their cakes were sweetened with honey.

Greek pancakes

Meals in ancient Greece were based around fish, home-baked bread and vegetables such as onions, beans, lentils, leeks and radishes. Chickens and pigeons were kept for their eggs and meat, and a cow or a few goats or sheep for milk and cheese. Pancakes like the ones in this project made handy snacks.

dried apricots

olives

raisins

◀ **Drying fruits**

Raisins (dried grapes) and apricots, and olives, were plentiful in the Mediterranean and used for cooking.

YOU WILL NEED
8 tbsp clear honey, spoon, small bowl, 3½oz flour, sieve, mixing bowl, fork, ⅞ cup (7oz) water, frying pan, sesame seeds, 1 tbsp olive oil, spatula, serving plate.

1 First measure the honey into a small bowl. Then make the pancake mix. Sieve the flour into a mixing bowl. Then, using a fork, stir the water into the flour. Mix into a runny paste.

2 Spoon the honey into the pancake mixture a little at a time. Mix it with a fork, making sure that the mixture is nice and smooth, and that there are no lumps.

3 Ask an adult to help you with the next two steps. Heat the frying pan. Sprinkle in the sesame seeds and cook them until they are brown. Set the seeds aside to cool.

4 Heat a tablespoon of olive oil in a frying pan. Pour a quarter of the pancake mixture into the frying pan. Cook on both sides for about four minutes until golden brown.

5 Serve the pancake on a plate. Sprinkle on a handful of sesame seeds and pour extra honey over the top. Cook the rest of the pancake mixture in the same way.

Pancakes were popular among theater-goers in ancient Greece. Stalls were set up around theaters to catch the crowds as they left.

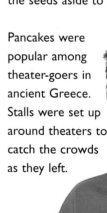

Roman honeyed dates

Many Roman town-dwellers lived in homes without kitchens. They ate takeout meals brought from the many food stalls and bars in town. Breakfast may only have been a quick snack of bread, honey and olives. Lunch, too, was a light meal, perhaps of eggs, or cold meats and fruit. The main meal of the day was *cena* (dinner). This might start with shellfish or a salad, followed by a main meal of roast pork, veal, chicken or goose with vegetables. Cena finished with a sweet course of fruit or honey cakes.

YOU WILL NEED

Chopping board, sharp knife, dates, hazlenuts, walnuts, pecans, almonds, pestle and mortar, salt, ¾ cup (6oz) honey, frying pan, wooden spoon, serving dish, a few fresh mint leaves.

1 Slit open the dates with the knife on the chopping board. Remove the stone inside. Be sure not to cut the dates completely in half and use the knife carefully.

2 Set aside the hazelnuts. Chop up the rest of the nuts. Use a pestle and mortar to grind them into smaller pieces. Stuff a small amount into the middle of each date.

3 Pour some salt onto the chopping board and lightly roll each of the stuffed dates in it. Make sure the dates are coated all over, but do not use too much salt.

4 Slowly melt the honey in a frying pan on a low heat. Lightly fry the dates for about 5 minutes, turning them with a wooden spoon. Ask an adult to help you use the stove.

5 Arrange the stuffed dates in a shallow serving dish. Sprinkle over the whole hazelnuts, some of the chopped nuts and a few fresh mint leaves. The dates are now ready to eat!

The Romans loved sweet dishes made from nuts and dates imported from North Africa. They also used dates to make sauces for savory fish dishes.

Indian chickpea curry

The diet of most people in ancient India depended on what plants were grown around them. In the areas of high rainfall, rice was the main food. In drier areas, people grew wheat and made it into bread.

Religion affected diet, too. Buddhists did not agree with killing animals, so they were vegetarians. Most Hindus became vegetarian, too. Hindus believed the cow was holy, so eating beef was forbidden. Muslims were forbidden to eat pork, although they did eat other meats. Chickpeas, peas, lentils and cheese provided healthy alternatives to meat.

The Indians used many spices in cooking to add flavor, to sharpen the appetite or aid digestion. Ginger, turmeric, cinnamon and cumin have been used from early times. Chillis were introduced from the Americas after the 1500s.

▲ **Staple food**

Rice cultivation has been the dominant agricultural activity in most parts of India since ancient times. The starchy, grain-like seeds form the main part of most Indian dishes. A rice plant's roots must be submerged in water, so a reliable irrigation system was essential if farmers were to obtain a good yield.

YOU WILL NEED

Knife, chopping board, small onion, 2 tbsp vegetable oil, wok, wooden spoon, 1½in cube of fresh ginger root, two cloves of garlic, ¼ tsp turmeric, 1lb tomatoes, 8oz cooked chickpeas, salt and pepper, 2 tbsp chopped cilantro, 2 tsp garam masala, cilantro for garnish, a lime.

1 Ask an adult to help you cook. Finely chop the onion. Heat the oil in a wok or frying pan. Fry the onion in the oil for two to three minutes until it is soft.

2 Finely chop the ginger and add it to the wok. Chop the garlic cloves and add them to the wok, too, along with the turmeric. Cook gently for another minute.

3 Peel the tomatoes, cut them in half and remove all the seeds. Roughly chop the tomatoes up and add them to the onion, garlic and spice mixture in the wok.

4 Add the cooked chickpeas to the pan. Gently bring the mixture to the boil, then simmer gently for around 10–15 minutes until the sauce has reduced to a thick paste.

5 Taste the curry and add salt and pepper as seasoning if required. The curry should taste spicy but not so hot that it burns your mouth – or those of your guests!

Add the chopped cilantro to the curry, along with the garam masala. Stir thoroughly. Garnish with a scattering of cilantro and serve with a slice of lime.

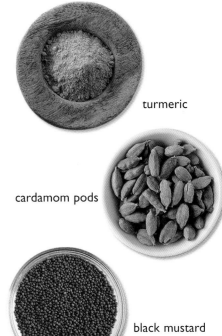

turmeric

cardamom pods

black mustard seeds

▲ Essential spices
Turmeric is ground from the root of a plant to give food an earthy flavor and yellow color. Black mustard seed has a smoky, bitter taste. Cardamom gives a musky, sugary flavor suitable for both sweet and savory dishes.

mango leaves

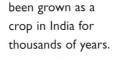

limes

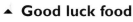

rice flour

▲ Good luck food
Various foods and plants were placed at the entrance of an Indian home for good luck. Rice-flour pictures were drawn on the step, and mango leaves and limes were hung above the door.

Chickpeas are an extremely popular ingredient in Indian cooking. They have been grown as a crop in India for thousands of years.

Chinese bean soup

Rice was the basis of most meals in ancient China, especially in the south where it was grown. It was often added to soup. People from the north made noodles and buns from wheat flour instead. They also made pancakes and dumplings, as well as lamb and duck dishes. For most people, however, meat was a luxury.

millet

rice

mung beans

sesame seeds

◄ **Cooking in China**
Mung beans, rice, millet and sesame seeds are all important additions to Chinese dishes and sauces.

YOU WILL NEED
Measuring cup, bowl, water, scales, 8oz aduki beans, 3 tsp ground nuts, 4 tsp short-grain rice, tangerine, saucepan, wooden spoon, 6oz sugar, liquidizer, sieve, serving bowls.

1 Measure out 1¾ pints of water. Weigh, wash and drain the beans, nuts and rice and put them in a bowl. Add the water and leave overnight to soak. Do not drain off the water.

2 Wash and dry the tangerine. Then carefully use your fingers to ease off the peel in one long, continuous strip. Leave the peel overnight to become hard and dry.

3 Put beans, rice and liquid into a saucepan. Add the peel and 2¼ cups (17oz) water. Ask an adult to help you bring the mixture to the boil. Cover the pan and simmer for two hours.

4 Use the scales to weigh out the sugar. When the water has boiled off and is just covering the beans, add the sugar. Simmer until the sugar has completely dissolved.

5 Remove and discard the tangerine peel. Leave the soup to cool. Then liquidize the mixture. Strain any lumps with a sieve. Pour the soup into bowls and serve.

Most peasant farmers lived on a simple diet. Red bean soup with rice was a typical meal.

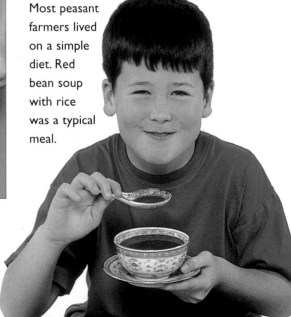

Japanese rice balls

Food in Japan has always been simple and healthy. The diet is based on rice, millet, wheat or barley, which is boiled, steamed or made into noodles. Many foods are flavored with soy sauce, made from fermented soya beans. Another nutritious soya product, tofu (beancurd), is made from soya beans softened and pulped in water. The pulp is formed into blocks and left to set.

seaweed

mussels

◂ **Treasures from the sea**

Japan is an island, so seafood, such as mussels and seaweed, is an important part of the Japanese diet.

YOU WILL NEED
7 cups Japanese rice, saucepan, sieve, wooden spoon, mixing bowls, 1 tbsp salt, chopping board, 1 tbsp black sesame seeds, ½ sheet yaki nori seaweed, knife, cucumber, serving dish.

1 Ask an adult to help you boil the rice. When the rice is cooked, drain it in the sieve but do not rinse it. The rice should remain sticky. Place the rice in one mixing bowl and salt in another.

2 Wash your hands thoroughly. Then wet the palms of both hands with cold water. Next, put a finger into the bowl of salt and rub a little onto your palms.

3 Place about one eighth of the rice on one hand. Use both your hands to shape the rice into a triangular shape. You should press firmly but not too hard.

4 Make seven more rice balls in the same way. When you have made them all, sprinkle some of the sesame seeds over each one to add some flavor to the rice balls.

5 Cut a strip of yaki nori seaweed into four pieces and wrap some of your rice balls in it. Put the *onigiri* on a serving dish and garnish them with sliced cucumber.

Rice was introduced from China in AD100 and remains the staple food of Japan.

Celtic cakes

In Celtic times, you would have had to watch how many oatcakes you ate. The Celts did not approve of people getting too fat. Roman writers reported that Celtic warriors were told not to let out their belts, but to lose weight when clothes around their waists became too tight. The Celts produced most of their own food on their farms. All they needed to buy were products such as salt.

apples

◄ **Home-grown fruits**

In Celtic times in northern Europe, many fruits were available that are familiar to us today.

YOU WILL NEED

8oz oatmeal, bowl, 3oz p flour, sieve, salt, wooden spoon, baking soda, 2oz butter, pan, water, heat-resistant glass, chopping board, rolling pin, glass, baking tray, wire tray.

1 Under adult supervision, preheat an oven to 425°F/Gas Mark 7. Put the oatmeal into the bowl. Sieve the flour into the bowl and add the salt. Mix all the ingredients with a wooden spoon.

2 Add the baking soda. Mix it in well and then put the bowl to one side. Melt the butter in a small pan over a low heat. Add it to the oat and flour mixture.

3 Boil some water and gradually add it to the oatmeal and flour mixture, straight from the kettle or in a heat-resistant glass. Stir well until you have a firm dough.

4 Turn the dough out onto a board sprinkled with a little oatmeal and flour. Roll the dough until it is about ⅜in thick. Use a glass to cut the dough into about 24 circles.

5 Place the circles of dough on a greased baking tray. Bake in an oven for about 15 minutes. Allow the oatcakes to cool on a wire tray before serving them.

Enjoy your oatcakes plain or eat them with butter, honey or cheese.

Viking bread

A typical Viking family ate twice a day. The food was usually prepared on a central hearth, although some large farmhouses had separate kitchens. Oats, barley and rye were made into bread and oatmeal. The hand-ground flour was often coarse and gritty. Poor people added split peas and bark to make it go further, and their teeth became worn down. Dough was mixed in large wooden troughs and baked in ovens or on stone griddles. Goat, beef and horse meat were roasted or stewed in cauldrons over a fire.

YOU WILL NEED

2 cups white bread flour, 3 cups whole-wheat flour, sieve, mixing bowl, 1 tsp baking powder, 1 tsp salt, 1 cup edible seeds, 2 cups warm water, wooden spoon or spatula, baking tray.

1 Sieve the flours into a bowl. Add the baking powder and salt. Stir half of the seeds into the bowl. Sunflower seeds give a crunchy texture, but you could use any other edible seeds.

2 Add two cups of warm water and stir the mixture with a wooden spoon or spatula. At this stage the mixture should become quite stiff and difficult to stir.

3 Use your hands to knead the mixture into a stiff dough. Before you start, dust your hands with some of the flour to stop the mixture sticking to them.

4 When the dough is well kneaded and no longer sticks to your hands, put it on a greased baking tray. Sprinkle the rest of your seeds over the top of the loaf.

5 Put the baking tray in a cold oven. Ask an adult to turn the oven to 375°F/Gas Mark 5. Cook the bread for one hour. Cooking the bread from cold will help the loaf to rise.

The Vikings put split peas in bread to add flavor and bulk, but sunflower seeds are just as tasty! Bread made from barley was most common, but wealthy Vikings ate loaves made from finer wheat flour.

Native American corn cakes

Tribes of North America have hunted, fished and gathered their own food from the earliest days. The Inuit fished from kayaks or through holes in the ice. Calusa tribes of the Southeast farmed the sea, sectioning off areas for shellfish. Tribes of the Northwest coast also harvested the sea. They therefore had little reason to develop farming, although they did cultivate tobacco.

For many peoples, however, farming was an important way of life. The Pueblos of the Southwest cultivated corn and made a thin bread, rather like the one ou can make. Tribes on the fertile east coast, such as the Secotan, set fire to land to clear it and then planted thriving vegetable gardens. As well as the staple corn, squash and beans, they grew berries, tomatoes, vanilla and asparagus. Archaeologists have found evidence of a tyoe of popcorn dating from 4000BC.

artichoke
plums

▲ Offerings to the dead
The Shawnee Feast of the Dead was held each year to honor the spirits of the dead tribal members. They would place luxurious fruits and food, such as artichokes and plums, on the graves and light candles all round.

seal
Inuit fisherman
Chipewyan canoe
Cree
beaver
Tsimshian
salmon
corn
Huron
Haida house
Sioux
Iroquois
Hopewell Mound
N
Paiute basket-maker
Cheyenne warrior hunting bison
Secotan
Navajo
Kiowa camp
Cherokee village of Echota
Apache
Comanche
Calusa
eagle

▲ Harvesting the land
The area and environment tribes lived in determined what they ate. Tribes of the Northwest who lived on the coast took their food from the sea. For many tribes on the fertile eastern coast, farming was an important way of life.

corn
squashes
mixed beans

▲ Vegetable crops
Corn was the staple food for most Native American tribes. Two other important vegetable crops were squashes and beans.

46

YOU WILL NEED

7oz corn tortilla flour or all-purpose flour, measuring scales, sieve, mixing bowl, pitcher, cold water, metal spoon, chopping board, rolling pin, frying pan, a little vegetable oil for cooking, honey.

1 Measure out 7oz of the corn tortilla flour or all-purpose flour using the measuring scales. Carefully sieve the flour into the mixing bowl. Fill the pitcher with cold water.

2 Slowly add the water to the flour in the mixing bowl. Add a little water at a time, stirring all the time as you pour, until the mixture forms into a stiff dough.

3 Using your hands, gently knead the mixture. Keep kneading the dough until it is not too sticky to touch. You may need to add a little more flour to get the consistency right.

4 Sprinkle flour over the board. Take the dough from the bowl and knead it on the floured chopping board for about ten minutes. Leave the dough to stand for 30 minutes.

5 Pull off a small lump of dough. Roll it between your hands to form a flattened ball. Repeat this process until you have made all the dough into flattened balls.

6 Keep kneading the dough balls until they form flat, round shapes. Finish them off by using the rolling pin to roll them into flat, thin cakes called tortillas.

7 Ask an adult to help you cook the tortillas. Heat a heavy frying pan or griddle. Gently cook the cakes in a little oil one by one until they are lightly browned on both sides.

Tortillas were usually eaten with savory food, but they also taste delicious with honey.

Aztec tortillas

Mesoamerican people usually ate their main meal around noon and had a smaller snack in the evening. Ordinary people's food was plain – but very healthy – as long as there was enough of it. Everyday meals were based on corn (which was ground down for tortillas), beans, vegetables and fruit. Peppers, tomatoes, pumpkins and avocados were popular, and the Aztecs also ate boiled cactus leaves. Soup made from wild herbs or seeds boiled in water was also a favorite. Meat and fish were luxuries. Deer, rabbit, turkey and dog were cooked for feasts, as well as frogs, lizards and turtles. The Aztecs also ate fish eggs and algae from the lakes.

tomato

avocado

▲ New food

Today, many Central American meals still include tomatoes, peppers, chilli peppers and avocados. These fruits and vegetables were first introduced to Europe and Asia in the years after the conquest of Mesoamerica.

mixed beans

prickly pear

▲ Vegetarian diet

Beans were an important part of the Mesoamerican diet. So was the fruit of the prickly pear cactus. The fine spines had to be carefully removed first!

◀ Floating gardens

Chinampas were very productive floating gardens. Layers of twigs and branches were sunk beneath the surface of a lake and weighted with stones. The government passed laws telling farmers when to sow seeds to ensure there would be a steady supply of vegetables for sale in the market.

YOU WILL NEED

Measuring scales, 8oz all purpose flour or corn flour, 1 tsp salt, mixing bowl, 1 tbsp butter, pitcher, 1½ cups cold water, teaspoon, rolling pin, chopping board, a little vegetable oil for frying, nonstick frying pan.

1 Weigh out all the ingredients. Mix the flour and salt together in a bowl. Rub the butter into the mixture until it looks like breadcrumbs. Then pour in the water a teaspoon at a time.

2 Use your hands to mix everything together until you have a loose mixture of dough. Do not worry if there is still some dry mixture around the sides of the bowl.

3 Knead the dough for at least ten minutes until it is smooth. If the dough on your hands gets too sticky, you could add a little plain flour to the bowl.

4 Tip the dough out of the bowl onto a floured chopping board. Divide it into egg-sized balls using your hands or a knife. You should have enough for about 12 balls.

5 Sprinkle the board and the rolling pin with a little plain flour to stop the dough from sticking. Then roll each ball of dough into a thin pancake shape called a tortilla.

6 Ask an adult to help you fry the tortillas using a nonstick frying pan. Fry each tortilla for one minute on each side. You can use a little oil in the pan if you want to.

You could eat your tortillas with a spicy bean stew or juicy tomatoes and avocados. In Aztec times, tortillas were cooked on a hot baking-stone.

Inca bean stew

The wealthiest members of Inca society entertained their visitors with banquets of venison, duck, fresh fish and tropical fruits, such as bananas and guavas. Honey was used as a sweetener. Peasants ate squash and other vegetables in a stew or soup like the one in the project, and added fish if it was available. Families kept guinea pigs for meat, but most of their food was based on a vegetarian diet. The bulk of any meal was made up of starchy foods. These were prepared from grains such as corn or quinoa, or from root crops such as potatoes, cassava or a highland plant called *oca*. A strong beer called *chicha* was made from corn.

cassava

sweet potatoes

▲ **Common crops**

Many of the world's common crops were first grown and then cultivated in the Americas. These include cassava and sweet potatoes.

chilli peppers

peanuts

▲ **Tropical taste**

Chilli peppers and peanuts are just two of a number of tropical crops that grow in the Americas.

◀ **A fertile land**

Corn was common across Central and South America. Potatoes and quinoa were grown in the area occupied by present-day Chile, Peru and Ecuador. Squashes and beans were cultivated mainly in Central America.

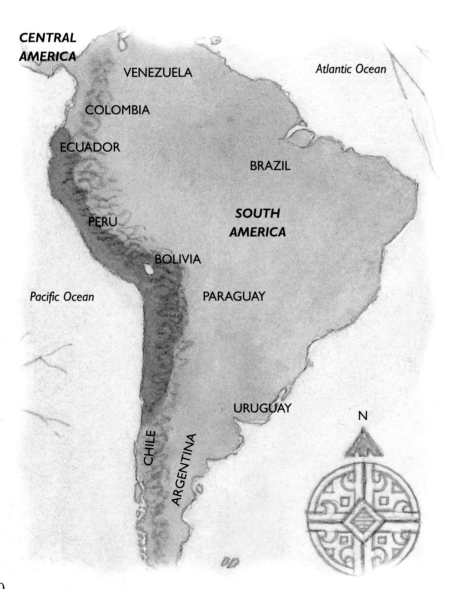

CENTRAL AMERICA

VENEZUELA

Atlantic Ocean

COLOMBIA

ECUADOR

BRAZIL

PERU

SOUTH AMERICA

BOLIVIA

Pacific Ocean

PARAGUAY

URUGUAY

N

CHILE

ARGENTINA

YOU WILL NEED

9oz dried haricot beans, bowl, cold water, sieve, large and medium pans, 4 tomatoes, knife, chopping board, 1¼lb pumpkin, 2 tbsp paprika, mixed herbs, salt, black pepper, 3¾oz corn.

1 Wash and then soak the beans in water for four hours. Drain and then put them into a large pan. Cover with water. Ask an adult to help you boil the beans. Simmer for two hours.

2 While the beans are cooking, chop up the tomatoes into fine pieces. Then peel the pumpkin and remove and discard the seeds. Cut the fleshy part of the pumpkin into ¾in cubes.

3 Ask an adult to help you heat 3½oz of water in a medium pan. Stir in the paprika and bring to the boil. Add the tomatoes and a pinch of mixed herbs. Season with salt and pepper.

4 Simmer for 15 minutes until the mixture is thick and well blended. Drain the beans and add them to the tomato mixture. Add the pumpkin and then simmer for 15 minutes.

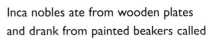

Inca nobles ate from wooden plates and drank from painted beakers called *keros*, but most peasants drank and ate from the dried, woody shells of gourds.

5 Add the corn and simmer the tomato mixture for an additional 5 minutes until the pumpkin has almost disintegrated and the stew is nice and thick.

6 Carefully taste the tomato and bean stew, and add more salt and pepper if you think it is necessary. Serve in bowls. Cornbread or tortillas would be an ideal accompaniment.

Medieval flan

It was quite usual to have a mixture of sweet and savory dishes in one course at a medieval castle feast. The flan you can make here mixes savory cheese with sugar and spice, all in one dish. Other sweet pies might have been made with cream, eggs, dates and prunes. In medieval times, food was often colored with vegetable dyes such as saffron, sandalwood or sometimes even gold. The pinch of saffron in the cream cheese mixture of this dish gives the flan a rich yellow color. Saffron is expensive because it comes only from the flowers of a type of Mediterranean crocus and is difficult to get hold of. For hundreds of years, it has been seen as a sign of wealth and status.

Remember to wash and clear up your mess when you have finished cooking. Before the days of cleaning products and dishwashers, dirty pots and pans were scoured clean using sand and soapy herbs.

▲ **Tasty titbits**

It was not considered to be good manners to feed the castle dogs and cats from the table, but leftover bones and scraps of food were usually tossed on the floor. People also spat on the floor (this was considered to be polite), which quickly became dirty and was not cleaned very often. Straw covered the floor and would be changed for new straw periodically.

YOU WILL NEED

Measuring scales, two mixing bowls, four small bowls, plate, egg cup, tea strainer, fork, whisk, spoon, chopping board, rolling pin, wax paper, 6in-diameter fluted pie pan, knife, two large eggs, pinch of saffron, hot water, 5¾oz cream cheese, 1 tbsp sugar, 1 tsp powdered ginger, salt, 9oz pack of ready-made unsweetened short pastry, flour.

1 Have all your bowls and utensils laid out and ready to use. Weigh out all the ingredients carefully using the scales. Place them in separate bowls on the work surface.

2 Break each egg in turn onto a plate. Place an egg cup over the yolk. Tip the plate over a bowl and discard the egg whites. Transfer the yolks into a bowl.

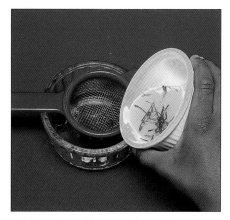

3 Put the saffron in a bowl. Heat some water and pour a little of it over the saffron. Leave until the water turns golden and then strain the liquid into another bowl.

4 Use a metal fork to mash up the cream cheese in a mixing bowl. Carry on blending until there are no lumps and the cream cheese is of a soft and creamy consistency.

5 Add the tablespoon of sugar to the egg yolks. Use a whisk to beat the egg and sugar together. Continue until the mixture has thickened a little.

6 Gradually add the cream cheese to the egg and sugar mixture. Use the whisk to gently beat in the cream cheese until it has completely blended with the egg and sugar.

7 Add the powdered ginger, salt and saffron water to the cream cheese and egg mixture. Stir all the ingredients thoroughly. Ask an adult to preheat the oven to 400–410°F/Gas Mark 6 or 7.

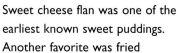

Sweet cheese flan was one of the earliest known sweet puddings. Another favorite was fried bread flavored with sugar and sherry.

8 Roll the pastry on a lightly floured board. Smear wax paper over the pie pan and cover with the pastry. Press the pastry into the edges of the pie pan and trim the excess pastry.

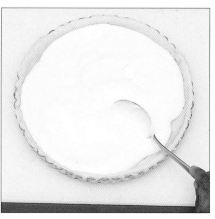

9 Spoon the cream cheese mixture over the pastry base and smooth it out to lay flat. Ask an adult to place the flan in the center of the preheated oven and bake for 20 to 30 minutes.

Halloween feast

Cook some scary food for a Halloween party on October 31. Then, the sun was said to be so low that the gates of the underworld were opened to let in the light. As the gates opened, demons and specters escaped onto Earth.

Cat and bat cookies

1 Scale up the bat and cat templates. Draw them onto the thick card, and then cut them out. You could make other shapes such as jack-o'-lanterns, pumpkins, witches' hats and ghosts.

2 Put the butter into a mixing bowl. (Take it out of the fridge in advance to soften it.) Add the sugar and stir with a wooden spoon until mixture is fluffy and creamy.

3 Add one beaten egg, the plain flour and a few drops of black food coloring to the bowl. Stir the mixture until it forms a stiff dough. Make sure the food coloring blends in well.

4 Roll the dough out onto a chopping board until it is about ⅜in thick. Place the cat and bat templates onto the dough and cut around them with a blunt knife.

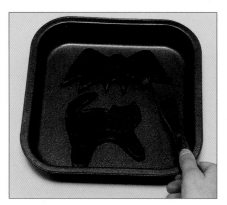

5 Roll out the leftover dough and cut out more bat and cat shapes. Place them onto a nonstick baking tray. Ask an adult to bake the animal cookies for 20 minutes at 374°F/Gas Mark 5.

6 When they are done, remove the cookies from the oven and place them on a wire tray. When cool, use red and green icing to add features such as eyes and noses.

Scary potato face

1 Ask an adult to bake a large baking potato. When it has cooled, use a knife to cut off the top. Then spoon out the insides into a mixing bowl. Add green food coloring and mix well.

2 Add the butter and grated cheese and season the potato mixture with salt and pepper. Mix thoroughly with a fork. Spoon the potato mixture back into the potato skin and keep it warm.

3 Use a knife to slice the carrot, red pepper and onion ends into strips for hair, mouth and eyebrows as shown above. Slice the sausage to make eyes. Sprinkle with grated orange cheese.

Ghoulish drink

1 You need one plastic straw for each drink you make. Use a glue brush to dab glue near one end of the straw. Fix a toy spider firmly in place. Leave to dry completely.

2 Put the glass onto a small plate. Put three of four tablespoons of ice cream in the glass. Mint chocolate chip looks good, because it is a ghoulish green color.

3 Pour a carbonated drink over the ice cream. A lime drink works well because it is a ghastly green color like the ice cream. Pour in enough so that the ice cream really froths up.

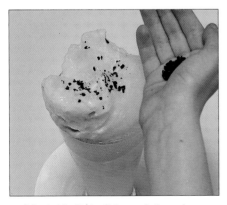

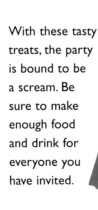

4 Sprinkle little flakes of chocolate over the top. You could add mini marshmallows or hundreds and thousands instead. Stick a decorative straw into each drink you make.

With these tasty treats, the party is bound to be a scream. Be sure to make enough food and drink for everyone you have invited.

Cowboy cookout

People were constantly on the move in the West. Native Americans followed herds of buffalo, settlers traveled in wagon trains and cowboys drove cattle. Everyone had to carry food with them and hunt animals for fresh meat.

Whatever food the cowboys carried with them was stored in their rolling kitchen, which was called the chuck wagon. One man had the job of cooking for all the others. This project shows you how to make the kind of meal a group of cowboys would have eaten on the trail.

▲ Hung out to dry
Native Americans hung strips of buffalo meat over poles in the open air. The Sun's heat dried and preserved the meat.

YOU WILL NEED

Two frying pans, cooking oil, garlic, wooden spoon, can of tomatoes, mild chilli powder, teaspoon, sieve, canned beans, stock cube, mixing bowl, 9oz all-purpose flour, 2oz cornmeal, salt, knife, warm water, chopping board, rolling pin, spatula.

1 Ask an adult to help you with your cowboy cookout. Heat a little oil in a frying pan. Crush two cloves of garlic and fry gently until soft and a light golden brown color.

2 Open the can of tomatoes and add the contents of the can to the garlic in the frying pan. Heat the tomatoes for a few moments until they are warmed through.

3 Stir one teaspoon of mild chilli powder into the tomato sauce. Taste it and add more chilli powder if you like, but remember that it will taste hotter when it is cooked.

4 Drain the liquid from the different cans of beans. Kidney beans, butter beans and pinto beans are a delicious combination. Stir the sauce and warm it through for a few minutes.

5 Crumble a stock cube into the tomato and chilli bean sauce and stir it in well. If the mixture becomes too dry, you may need to add a little hot water from a kettle.

6 Cook the bean sauce over a low heat for about ten minutes. Remove it from the stove, and leave it to one side. You can now make the tortillas for your cowboy feast.

7 Add the flour, cornmeal and a pinch of salt into the bowl and pour in a little warm water. Gradually add more and more water until the mixture forms into a stiff dough.

8 Sprinkle some flour over a chopping board and vigorously knead the dough until it feels stretchy and elastic. If the dough is too dry, try adding some more water to it.

9 Divide the dough mixture into six equal portions. Use your hands to shape each one into a ball. Then coat the outside of each ball lightly with a little flour.

10 Dust the chopping board with more flour. Using a rolling pin dusted with flour, roll out each ball into a flat circle. You should try to roll each one as thin as you possibly can.

You might like to invite a few friends over for this delicious cowboy feast.
Serve your tortillas on tin plates, just like the ones used by real cowboys.

11 Heat some oil in the second frying pan. Place one dough circle, called a tortilla, into the pan. When the edges curl, use a spatula to flip it over to cook on the other side.

12 When each tortilla is cooked, put it on a plate. Reheat the tomato and chilli bean sauce. Spoon some over half the tortilla. Fold over the other half. Serve immediately.

ARCTIC WORLD

ARCTIC WORLD

North
Sea

VIKING LANDS

North
America

CELTIC LANDS

AZTEC & MAYA
EMPIRES

Gulf of
Mexico

Atlantic Ocean

Caribbean
Sea

Central
America
(Mesoamerica)

Pacific Ocean

INCA
EMPIRE

Andes Mountains

South
America

Cape Horn

ARCTIC WORLD

ARCTIC WORLD

VIKING LANDS

Baltic Sea

Europe

ROME

ANCIENT GREECE

Black Sea

Caspian Sea

Asia

Mediterranean Sea

ANCIENT EGYPT

MESOPOTAMIA

CHINA

JAPAN

Sea of Japan

Persian Gulf

ANCIENT INDIA

South China Sea

Red Sea

Arabian Sea

Bay of Bengal

Africa

Indian Ocean

Australia

Cape of Good Hope

Glossary

A

agriculture the preparation of land in order to grow crops or raise animal livestock.

amphora A large, narrow necked Greek or Roman jar with a handle on either side. Amphorae were used to store liquids such as wine or oil.

Anno Domini (AD) A system used to calculate dates after the supposed year of Jesus Christ's birth. Anno Domini dates in this book are prefixed AD up to the year 1000, for example, AD521. After 1000 no prefixes are used.

archaeology The scientific study of the past, which involves looking at the remains of ancient civilizations.

Arctic A vast, frozen area surrounding the North Pole.

artefact An object that has been preserved from the past.

atrium A central court or entrance hall in a Roman house.

Assyrian An inhabitant of the Assyrian Empire. From 1530–612BC, Assyria occupied east of the Mediterranean Sea to Iran, and from the Persian Gulf to the mountains of eastern Turkey.

Aztec Mesoamerican people who lived in northern and central Mexico. They were at their most powerful between 1350 and 1520.

B

banquet An elaborate meal where there are usually several guests.

Before Christ (BC) A system that is used to calculate dates before the supposed year of Jesus Christ's birth. These dates are calculated in reverse. For example, 2000BC is longer ago than 200BC.

Bronze Age A period in human history, between 3000 and 1000BC, when tools and weapons were made from bronze.

C

Celt A member of one of the ancient peoples that inhabited most parts of Europe from around 750BC to AD1000.

ceramics The art and technique of making pottery.

climate The general weather pattern of a place, year by year.

circa (*c.*) A symbol used to mean 'approximately', when the exact date of an event is not known e.g. *c.*1000BC.

citizen A Roman term used to describe a free person with the right to vote.

D

dowel A thin cylindrical length of wood. Dowelling is available from hardware stores.

E

earthquake A succession of vibrations that shake the earth's surface, caused by shifting movement in the earth's crust.

engrave To carve letters or designs onto stone, wood or metal.

F

festival A day or period of celebration, often one that is a tradition.

figurine A small carved or moulded fugure that usually represents a human form.

firing The process of baking clay or glass paste in a kiln to harden it and make it waterproof.

fresco A picture painted on a wall while the plaster is still damp.

G

gilding The process of applying a thin layer of gold to metal or pottery.

H

harvest The gathering in of ripened crops, usually in the late summer or early autumn.

hieroglyph A picture symbol used in ancient Egypt to represent an idea, word or sound.

hilt The handle of a sword.

Hinduism A world religion characterized by the worship of several gods and a belief in reincarnation.

hominid Humans and their most recent ancestors.

Homo sapiens The Latin species name for modern humans. The words *Homo* and *sapiens* together mean 'wise man'.

hospitality The friendly welcome and entertainment of guests or strangers, which usually includes offering them food and drink.

hunter-gatherer People who hunt wild animals for their meat and gather plants for food as a way of life.

I

ice age Several periods in Earth's history when the average temperature of the atmosphere decreased and large parts of the Earth's surface were covered with snow and ice. The most significant ice age was between 30,000 and 12,000 BC.

igloo A dome-shaped Inuit shelter built from blocks of snow and ice.

Inca A member of an indigenous South American civilization living in Peru before the Spanish conquest.

indigenous Native or originating from a certain place.

inscribed Lettering, pictures or patterns carved into a hard material such as stone or wood.

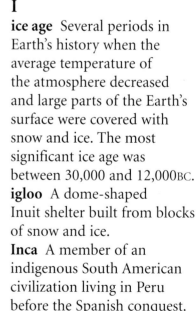

insulate to surround a house with a material that prevents or slows down the flow of heat, making the house warmer.

Inuit The native people of the Arctic and regions of Greenland, Alaska and Canada.

Iron Age The period when iron became the main metal used for producing tools and weapons. The Iron Age began around 1200BC.

iron ore Rock that contains iron in a raw, natural form.

Islam A world religion founded in the 7th century AD by the prophet Mohammed.

K

kanji The picture symbols based on Chinese characters that were used for writing Japanese before about AD800.

kayak A one-person Inuit canoe powered by a double-bladed paddle. The wooden or bone frame is covered with sealskin.

kiln An oven or furnace used for firing bricks or pottery.

L

legion The main unit of the Roman army made up only of Roman citizens.

legislation Making laws.

livestock Animals that are kept for the production of meat, milk, wool etc or for breeding

M

Maya An ancient civilization native to Mesoamerica.

medieval A term describing people, events and objects from a period in history known as the Middle Ages.

Mesoamerica A geographical area made up of the land between Mexico and Panama in Central America.

Mesopotamia An ancient name for the fertile region between the Tigris and Euphrates rivers in the Middle East.

Middle Ages Period in history that lasted from around AD800 to 1400.

mosaic A design or piece of work formed by fitting together lots of small pieces of coloured stone, glass, etc.

N

Native Americans The indigenous peoples of the Americas.

neolithic The New Stone Age. The period when people began to farm but were still using stone tools.

P

papier mâché Pulped paper mixed with glue, moulded into shape while wet and left to dry.

porcelain The finest quality of pottery. Porcelain is made with a fine clay called kaolin and baked at a high temperature.

prehistoric The period in history before written records were made.

pyramid A huge, stone tomb, square at the base with a pointed top, built to house the mummy of an Egyptian pharaoh.

R

ramparts The defensive parapets on top of castle walls.

relief A sculpture carved from a flat surface such as a wall.

roundhouse A circular house that the celts lived in.

S

shinden A single-storey Japanese house.

Shrine A place of worship or a container for holy relics such as bones.

society All the classes of people living in a particular community or country.

staple food The major part of the diet. For example, rice was the staple food of people in ancient India.

Stone Age The first period in human history in which people made their tools and weapons out of stone.

T

template A piece of card cut in a particular design and used as a pattern when cutting out material.

temple A building used for worship or other spiritual rituals.

tesserae Coloured tiles made of stone, pottery or glass and pressed into soft cement to form mosaics.

teepee A conical tent made up of skins stretched over a framework of wooden poles. Teepees are still used by some Native American tribes.

V

veranda A sheltered terrace attached to a house.

Viking One of the Scandinavian peoples who lived by sea raiding in the early Middle Ages.

villa A Roman country house, usually part of an agricultural estate.

Index